Favorite Fairy Tales

Rumpelstiltskin

Retold by Rochelle Larkin   Illustrated by Nan Brooks

CREATIVE CHILD PRESS
is a registered trademark of Playmore Inc.,
Publishers and Waldman Publishing Corp., New York, N.Y.

Once upon a time there lived a miller who had a beautiful daughter. He was very proud, and he wanted her to be much more than a miller's daughter. So he went to the king and told him he had a daughter who could spin straw into gold.

Now, the king was as greedy as the miller was proud, so they struck a bargain. The miller's daughter came to live at the castle, where she was put into a room heaped with straw. "Spin this into gold," said the king, "and you'll be queen. If not, you will die."

The miller's daughter was left alone. All night long she cried. She could barely spin flax into cloth, let alone straw into gold.

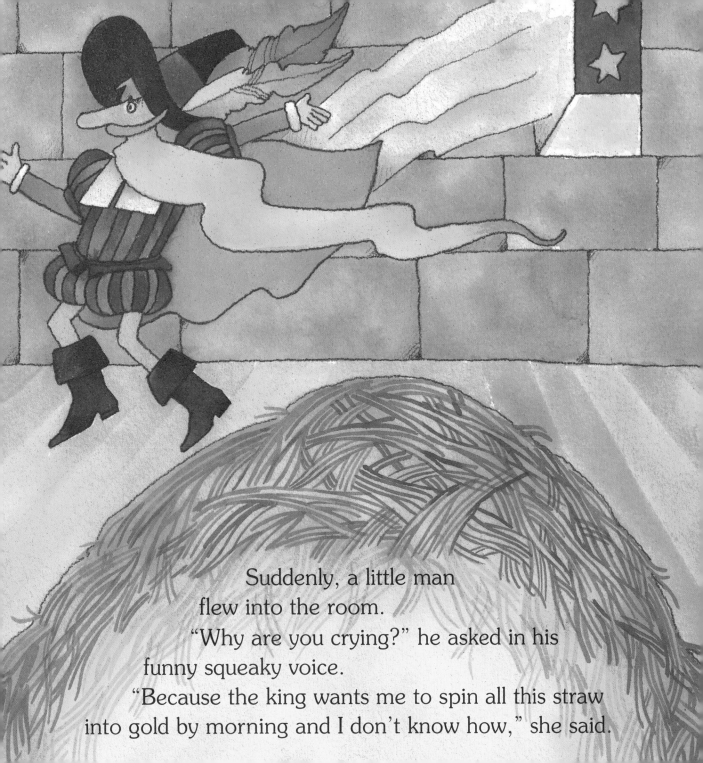

Suddenly, a little man
flew into the room.
"Why are you crying?" he asked in his
funny squeaky voice.
"Because the king wants me to spin all this straw
into gold by morning and I don't know how," she said.

"What will you give me to do it?" the little man asked.

"I have very little," the miller's daughter answered. "But you can have this ring."

"It's not much, but I'll do it," said the little man.

When the king came in the next morning and saw the room piled high with gold, he was both pleased and astonished.

"Unbelievable," he said. "You must do it again." And the miller's daughter was put into a bigger room with even more straw.

Again, the little man came to her aid.

"Help me," she pleaded, "or I will lose my life."

"When you are queen," said the little man, "and you will be, you will give me your firstborn child."

"Yes, yes, anything you want," said the miller's daughter.

When the king saw all the gold that had been spun that night, he married the miller's daughter. Now she was the queen.

When a baby prince was born to them, the king and queen were as happy as could be. All of the queen's fears were forgotten until one morning when the strange little man flew in at the window to remind her of her promise.

"Oh no!" cried the queen. "You can't take my baby from me.
You mustn't!" But nothing she offered him made the little man
change his mind.

   At last he gave in. "If you can guess my name in three days,"
he said, "you may keep the child. But three days, mind you."
And with that, out the window he flew.

The queen was more frightened than before. She couldn't tell the king about the gold, and couldn't bear to lose her child.

She sent for the captain of the castle. "You must search high and low," she said. "Find me the strangest names you can."

The captain searched through all the northern part of the
kingdom and brought a list to the queen.

The morning came, and the little man flew in the window again.
"Well, do you have it?" he demanded.

The queen began. "Is your name Maxey, Jaxey, or Gullfaxi?"
"No!" roared the little man.
"Is it Kenny, Lenny, or Benny?" asked the queen.
"No!" shouted the little man.

The captain went out again, searching the southern part of the kingdom. He listened carefully to all the names he heard and wrote them all down.

Next morning, the queen was ready for the little man.
"Is your name Ingnozel, Bingnozel, or Stringnozel?" she asked.
"No, no, and no!" he said. "You'll never guess!"

The captain went out to search the middle part of the kingdom, but he had heard all the names before. He was about to go to the queen with this sad news when a strange noise caught his ear.

Down at the entrance to a nearly hidden cave, he saw the strange little man doing a little dance and singing to himself.

"Oh, tomorrow the child I shall claim," he sang as he hopped about on one foot, "sure as Rumpelstiltskin is my name!"

The captain wrote it down
and hurried back to the queen.

When he described the little man, the queen knew she was saved.

Next morning, in he flew.
"Give me the child," he said to the queen.

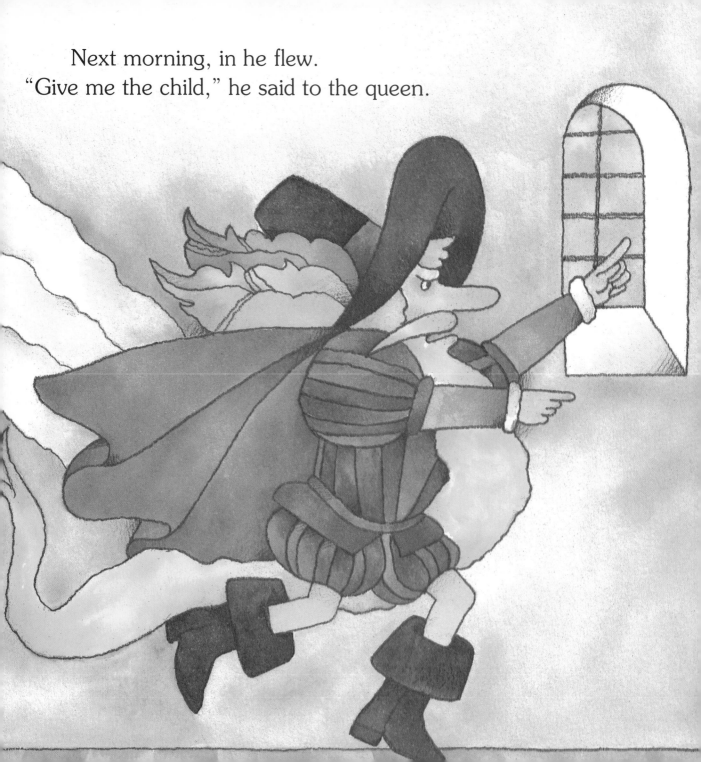

"Is your name John?" she asked with a smile.

"Of course not!" he snapped. "What's unusual about the name John?"

"Is it Peter?" asked the queen.

"Give me the child!" the little man shouted.

The queen smiled again.

"Is it Rumpelstiltskin?" she asked.

"You guessed! You guessed!" the little man shouted, stamping with both feet on the floor.

In fact, he stamped so hard that the floor opened right up and swallowed him whole.

Rumpelstiltskin disappeared completely. He was never seen again.
The king, the queen, and the little prince lived happily ever after.